Adam & Eve in Paradise

also by Eça de Queirós

FROM NEW DIRECTIONS

Eça de Queirós

Adam & Eve in Paradise

translated from the Portuguese
by Margaret Jull Costa

A NEW DIRECTIONS
PAPERBOOK ORIGINAL

Originally published in Portuguese
as *Adão e Eva no Paraíso*

Manufactured in the United States of America
First published as New Directions Paperbook 1620 in 2025

Library of Congress Control Number: 2024053310

2 4 6 8 9 7 5 3 1

New Directions Books are published for James Laughlin
by New Directions Publishing Corporation
80 Eighth Avenue, New York 10011

ADAM & EVE
IN PARADISE

Chapter I

Adam, the Father of Mankind, was created on the twenty-eighth day of October at two o'clock in the afternoon …

Or so, very solemnly, declares that most learned and most eminent fellow, James Ussher, Bishop of Meath, Archbishop of Armagh, and Chancellor of St Patrick's Cathedral, in his *Annales veteris et novi testamenti*.

The Earth only came into existence when Light was created on the twenty-third day, that morning of mornings. But it was no longer the same gray, soupy, primordial Earth, steeped in muddy waters, wrapped in a thick, choking mist, with a few stiff trunks sticking up here and there, bearing a single leaf, a single bud—it was not a solitary, silent place, with every form of life hidden away or dimly revealed by the stirrings of certain obscure gelatinous creatures, colorless and almost formless, in the depths of the mud. No! During the genesic days of the twenty-sixth and the twenty-seventh, the whole thing had been finished, furnished, and adorned, purely to give the Chosen One the welcome he deserved. On the twenty-eighth day, the Earth appeared in all its perfection, with all the accoutrements and ornaments enumerated in the Bible, the green leaves of ripening wheat, *perfecto*, the trees heavy with fruit and flowers, the fish swimming in the shining seas, the birds flying through the still air, the animals grazing on the lush hills, the streams watering the Earth, the fire stored and waiting in the bosom of the stone, along with the crystal and the onyx and the fine gold from the land of Havilah ...

In those days, my friends, the Sun still revolved around the Earth. The Earth was young and beautiful and God's favorite. The Sun had not yet submitted to the majestic immobility imposed on it later—provoking many a frown and a sigh from the Church—by Master Galileo, when he, in his orchard, right next to the convent of San Matteo in Florence, raised one finger and pointed. Then the Sun still ran amorously around the Earth, like the bridegroom in the *Song of Songs*, who, in the more lascivious days of his desire, ran tirelessly up the mountain of myrrh, skipping more lightly than the roe deer of Gilead, to embrace his Beloved and bathe her in the fiery glow of his eyes, glinting like rock salt with fecund impatience. Now, in the dawn of that twenty-eighth day, according to Ussher's magisterial calculations, the Sun—still very young, with no freckles or wrinkles, no thinning of its flaming hair—had enwrapped the Earth in a continuous, insatiable caress of heat and light for a whole eight hours. When that eighth hour flickered and fled, a confused feeling, a mix of dread and glory, ran through the whole of Creation, sending a shiver through grasses and trees alike, making the fur of wild beasts prickle and the backs of the mountains rise up, hastening the babbling rush of springs, and setting porphyry glittering ever more brightly. Then, in the dense, dark forest, a certain Being slowly loosened its grip on the branch on which it had been perched during that centuries-long morning, slid down the ivy-clad trunk, placed its two feet firmly on the soft, mossy ground and stood erect; then it swung its two free arms and took one long stride, and, suddenly aware of how different it was from the other animals, it had the most astonishing thought: it *existed*, and it did indeed exist! It had been created, in that instant, by God, its protector. And filled with superior life, having left his previous treelike state of unconsciousness, Adam strode toward Paradise.

He was a truly alarming sight. His whole large, sturdy body was covered in curly, glossy hair, apart from his elbows and his rough knees, where it grew more thinly, revealing a weather-beaten hide the color of dull copper. Above his pointed ears, a sparse, reddish mane of hair sprouted up from his flat, wrinkled, sloping cranium. His jutting jaw, the great crevice that opened up between his protruding snout-like lips, housed sharp fangs, perfect for tearing flesh and crushing bone. And beneath his deep-set brows, edged with thick fur—much as a bramble forms a hedge around the opening of a cave—his round, amber-yellow eyes darted ceaselessly to and fro, wide with anxiety and fear. No, our venerable Father was certainly not a pleasant sight when, on that autumn morning, Jehovah tenderly helped him down from his Tree! And yet despite the fear and dread in those round, amber-yellow eyes, there shone in them a superior beauty—the Intelligent Energy that was stumblingly leading him, on bowed legs, out of the forest where he had spent his centuries-long morning leaping and shrieking through the high branches.

However (if the anthropology textbooks do not deceive us), Adam's first human steps toward the destiny awaiting him among the four rivers of Eden, were not taken with great alacrity and confidence. Still under the spell of the forest, he moved clumsily over the leafy ground thick with ferns and begonias, savoring the touch of the heavy clusters of flowers bedewing his fur, and stroking the long white beards of Spanish moss that hung from the trunks of oak and teak where once he had enjoyed the sweet delights of irresponsibility. From the boughs that, through long ages, had so generously fed and cradled him, he still picked juicy berries and the tenderest of shoots. To cross the streams, which, after the rainy season, flowed sparkling and whispering through the whole forest, he would still swing from an occasional strong, orchid-entwined liana, making the same indolent, arching leap. And I fear that, when the breeze rustled through that thick foliage, laden with the warm, acrid smell of the female apes crouched high above, the splayed nostrils of the Father of Mankind did still dilate and from his hairy chest came a sad, hoarse grunt.

And yet on he walked. His yellow eyes, in which there was just a flicker of desire, peered probingly through the branches, seeking the world he both wanted and—already hearing the violent, rancorous roar of battle—feared. And as the leafy shade lightened, there emerged from within his fledgling mind, like the dawn light penetrating a burrow, a sense of the different Forms and the different Life that animated them. This rudimentary understanding, however, brought our venerable Father nothing but bewilderment and terror. The very proudest Traditions agree that when Adam first entered the plains of Eden, he trembled and cried like a small child lost in the crowd at some noisy village celebration. And we would be right in thinking that, of all those Forms, he found none so troubling as the very trees in which he had lived, now that he recognized them as so utterly unlike him, beings trapped in an inertia quite at odds with his energy. Freed now from his Animal self and on his way to Becoming Human, he saw that the trees that had been his sweet and entirely natural refuge resembled a sad, degrading prison. And those twisted branches hindering his progress, were they not strong arms reaching out to clutch and pull and keep him in the leafy heights? And the rustling whisper pursuing him, composed of the angry stirring of every leaf, was it not the whole indignant forest demanding the return of its centuries-old inhabitant? Perhaps Man's first struggle with Nature was born out of that strange fear. Whenever a long branch brushed against him, our Father would doubtless have held out desperate hands to fend it off and escape its clutches. During these abrupt encounters, he must often have lost his balance and landed with both hands on the ground or on a rock, regressing to his former bestial posture and to the unconscious life, much to the forest's triumphant and clamorous delight! With what haste and effort did he then regain his upright human posture, detaching his hairy arms from the brute Earth and thus freeing them up for the immense task of Becoming Human! A sublime effort in which he roared and gnawed at the hated roots and, who knows, lifted his shining, amber eyes to the heavens, where he had a vague sense that Someone was protecting him, someone who was, in fact, helping him to his feet.

From each of those falls, our Father emerged more human and more our Father. There was a consciousness now, a fast-growing rationality, in the ponderous steps with which he uprooted himself from his arboreal limbo, tearing his way through the tangle of creepers, forging a path through the dense vegetation, waking up tapirs asleep beneath monstrous mushrooms or startling a stray young bear who, feet propped against an elm tree, was devouring, half-drunk, the grapes of this abundant autumn.

Adam finally emerged from the dark forest, and screwed up his amber eyes against the dazzling light of Eden.

At the foot of the hill where he paused lay a disorderly, somber abundance of vast, glowing meadows (if the Traditions do not exaggerate). A river sprinkled with islands flowed slowly through them, creating the large, fertile pools that water the fields where lentils or rice were perhaps already growing. Glinting marble rocks blushed warm and pink. From among the forests of cotton plants, white and curly as foam, rose hillsides covered in magnolias of an even more splendid white. Beyond, the snow crowned a mountain with a radiant halo of sanctity and filled the crevices on its flanks with a glittering filigree. Silent flames of light darted from other mountains. Disheveled palm trees leaned precariously over the edge of escarpments, staring into the deep. The mist dragged its soft, luminous lace over the surface of the lakes. And the sparkling sea around the edges of the world enclosed everything like a ring of gold. In this fertile space the whole of Creation trembled with the force, grace, and vigorous health of its five-day-old youth, still warm from the hands of its Creator. Huge herds of auburn-haired aurochs grazed majestically in grass high enough to conceal the ewe and her lamb. Fearsome, bearded oxen did battle with giant deer, locking horns and antlers with the dry crack of oaks felled by the wind. A herd of giraffes nibbled away at the tenderest leaves at the tremulous tops of a stand of mimosas. Huge rhinoceroses, with urgent flocks of birds helpfully pecking them clean of insects, lay in the shade of the tamarinds. Every attack by a tiger provoked a furious flight of haunches and horns and manes, interspersed by the light, graceful leaps of the antelopes. A tall, erect palm tree was bent low beneath the weight of the boa constrictor winding around it. Sometimes, between two rocks, the shaggy mane and magnificent face of a lion could be seen gazing serenely up at the vast radiance of the Sun. In the blue distance, enormous condors, wings outspread, drifted and dozed among the white and pink wake left by the herons and flamingos. High on the hill opposite, a slow, mountainous caravan of mastodons passed by, the rough hair on their backs tousled by the wind, their trunks swaying between their scythe-like tusks.

This is how the most ancient of chronicles describe that most ancient of Edens, which existed in the grasslands of the Euphrates, or possibly in darkest Ceylon, or among the four clear rivers that now water Hungary, or even in the blessed land where our own dear Lisbon warms its old bones in the sun, weary of adventures and sea voyages. But who can guarantee the existence of those forests and those creatures, given that, since that twenty-fifth day of October filling Paradise with autumnal splendor, more than seven times seven hundred thousand brief but very full years have passed over the speck of dust that is our world? What is certain is that a large bird walked past a terrified Adam. A gray bird, bald and pensive, with ruffled feathers like the petals of a chrysanthemum, was hopping about on one foot while gripping a bundle of leaves and twigs in the other. Our venerable Father, Adam, furrowing his dusky brow in an effort to understand, was astonished to see that bird very gravely putting the finishing touches to a cabin beneath the shelter of an azalea bush in flower! And it was a very solid cabin, complete with smooth mud floor, posts and beams made of sturdy pine and beech-wood, a secure roof of dried grass, and, in the wall made of closely woven ivy stems, an opening for a window! However, on that afternoon, the Father of Mankind still could not grasp the meaning of it all.

Then, without leaving the safe bounds of the sheltering forest, he walked cautiously, slowly over to the broad river, scenting on the air the smell, new to him, of the plump herbivores of the plain. With his fists pressed tightly to his hairy chest, Adam was torn between feeling thrilled by such resplendent Nature and terrified by the wild rumblings and roarings of those never-before-seen beings. Inside him, though, ceaselessly bubbling up from the *source sublime*, was the Energy urging him to haul himself out of that crass brutish state and make an effort—an effort that was almost painful because already almost conscious—to try out the Gifts that would establish his supremacy over that incomprehensible Nature and free him from his fear. In his surprise at each one of Eden's unexpected apparitions—animals, fields, snowcapped mountains, vast radiant landscapes—Adam uttered a few hoarse exclamations, liberating cries, stammered calls, in which, instinctively, he reproduced other voices, yelps and songs and even the bumbling grunts of animals, even the roar of rushing water ... And in Adam's inchoate memory, those sounds remain linked to the sensations they provoked, and so the squeal that escaped him when he came across a kangaroo carrying its brood inside a pocket in its stomach, would spring from his protruding lips whenever he saw other kangaroos running away from him and vanishing into the dark shade cast by the cinnamon trees. The Bible, with its innocent, simplistic, oriental tendency to exaggerate, tells how Adam, the moment he entered Eden, immediately gave names to the animals and the plants, with as much certainty and erudition as if he were writing the Lexicon of Creation, half Buffon with his ornate cuffs, and half Linnaeus with his spectacles. Not at all. The names were merely groans, coarse but nonetheless worthy of respect, because they took root in his nascent consciousness like the crude roots of that Word through which he became truly human, and thus simultaneously sublime and absurd.

And we might well think proudly that, as he walked along the banks of the Edenic river, our Father—moved by what he *was* and by how different he was from every other being—was affirming himself, becoming an individual, as he beat on his sonorous breast and roared proudly: *Eheu! Eheu!* Then, with shining eyes, he gazed long and lingeringly down that long river flowing slowly into the beyond, trying to give voice to his sense of this astonishing space, and uttering a thoughtful, greedy grumble: *Lhlã! Lhlã!*

Chapter II

The calm, noble, magnificently fertile river of Paradise flowed around islands almost sunk beneath the weight of lush vegetation, every island alive and echoing with the clamorous cries of cockatoos. And as he trudged wearily along the bank, Adam could already feel the lure of those disciplined waters meandering on their lively way, the same attraction his children would one day feel when they realized that the river was their good servant, restoring order and providing food, irrigation, and transport. However, there were still many strange terrors that sent him darting for shelter beneath the willows and the poplars! On other islands, edged with fine pink sand, leathery-skinned crocodiles lay stretched out on their bellies, yawning idly, opening wide their great jaws in the tepid, lazy afternoon, and filling the air with the smell of musk. Fat, glossy water snakes zigzagged, tails up, through the reedbeds, fixing Adam with a furious stare, flicking their tongues in and out and hissing. And our Father would surely have been horrified by the sight of the huge turtles, which, in this just-begun World, were making their slow, meek way across the new fields. He did feel drawn, though, to one curious sight, and almost slithered down the muddy slope to where the fringe of water rubbed and lapped. Crossing the wide river, a long, black line of aurochs, horns held high, thick beards afloat, were serenely swimming to the farther shore full of golden fields where the ears of civilized corn and barley might already have been ripening. Our venerable Father watched that slow line of aurochs and watched the shining river too, filled with a vague desire to also cross over to those distant fields full of shining grasses. When he plunged one hand into the water, into the strong current that tugged at him, as if to draw him in and initiate him, he grunted and hastily withdrew his hand, before stumbling clumsily on, crushing underfoot the fresh wild strawberries spattering the grass with red, not even noticing their sweet scent ... Shortly afterward, he stopped to observe a flock of birds perched high up on a guano-striped rock; beaks at the ready, they were staring down into the churning waters. What were those white herons watching for? Why, for the shoals of beautiful fish that came leaping over the rocks, gleaming in the pale foam. And suddenly, with a great flapping of white wings, one heron, then another, flashed across the sky, diving in and emerging with a wriggling, glinting fish in its beak. Our venerable Father pensively scratched himself. Surrounded by the sheer abundance of the river, he, in his base greed, also fancied catching some prey, and so he reached out and caught a few crunchy insects as they buzzed past, sniffing them before biting into them. However, nothing so astonished the First Man as the sight of a large, half-rotten tree trunk floating down the river, with, seated confidently and elegantly at one end, two silky, russet-colored creatures with sharp noses and fluffy, presumptuous tails. In order to follow and observe them, he—an enormous, ungainly figure—ran eagerly after them. And his eyes shone, as if he could already sense the natural slyness of those creatures perched on a tree trunk and drifting down the river of Paradise in the cool evening air.

Meanwhile, the water beneath him had grown shallower, murkier, more sluggish. There were no lush green islands now, nor did the water lap the shores of luxuriant pastures. Off in the limitless distance, steeped in mist, he could glimpse deserted wildernesses, across which rolled a slow, hot wind. Our venerable Father's feet slipped and slithered down soft banks, stumbled over fallen branches, through alluvial swamps, where, to his intense horror, enormous frogs were furiously croaking. The river then became lost in a vast lake, dark and desolate— all that remained of the waters over which the Spirit of Jehovah once hovered. A human sadness gripped our Father's heart. In the midst of the great bubbles gurgling up from the smooth glossy surface of that grim water, hideous snouts, dripping with green slime, kept poking out, bellowing loudly, then sinking down again as if sucked under by the viscous mud. And when, from among the tall black reeds staining the scarlet evening hour, there arose a raucous cloud of voracious horseflies that immediately attacked him, Adam fled blindly away, skidding in the sticky gravel, grazing his skin on the rough, white, windblown thistles, sliding down a bank of shingle and pebbles to the fine sand below. Panting, his large ears twitched as he listened to the vast murmur coming from beyond the dunes, rolling, breaking and rolling back … The sea. Our Father crossed the pale dunes and there before him lay the Sea!

Then came an overwhelming feeling of fear. Wildly beating his chest with his fists, he retreated to a spot where three pine trees, bare and dead, offered him his hereditary refuge. Why were those green waves, each one topped with foam, ceaselessly rising and advancing threateningly toward him, only to hurl themselves, crumbling, hissing, and abjectly slavering, onto the sand? Meanwhile the rest of that vast expanse of water remained almost motionless, as if dead, like a great pulsating pool of blood, blood that must have fallen from a wound in the round, red Sun, which was already bleeding into a sky that bore the purple marks of several deep wounds. Beyond the milky mist covering the lagoons and beyond the salty pools formed by the tide when it rose and spread over the sands, a mountain was sending out flames and smoke. Meanwhile, the green waves of green water continued to advance before him and break and boom, scattering the beach with seaweed, shells, and glossy white jellyfish.

The whole sea was filling up with life! Huddled beneath his pine tree, our venerable Father kept shooting restless, nervous glances to right and left—at the rocks covered in algae where great fat seals reclined majestically; at the fountains of water rising up toward the purple clouds and falling back in the form of radiant rain; a lovely armada of conches—huge white, pearly conches—sailing windward and elegantly circumventing the cliffs … Adam stood there, astonished, unaware that those were Ammonites, and that, after him, no other man would see that gleaming, rosy armada sailing the world's seas. Even while he was admiring this sight, perhaps with a first sense of the beauty of things, the furrowed sea turned white, and the whole marvelous fleet went under! With one gentle leap, the seals tumbled into the deep waves. And a shudder of terror ran through everything, a terror that came from the sea, so intense that a whole rookery of albatrosses, safely installed on a steep slope, flew off, shrieking with fear.

Our venerable Father gripped one branch of his pine tree, and fearfully scanned the vast, now deserted scene. Then, in the distance, beneath the glow of the warily sinking Sun, a huge back slowly emerged from the waters, looking like a very long hill covered with sharp, black splinters of rock. And it was coming toward him, preceded by a tumult of whirling, bursting bubbles, from among which emerged, at last, a monstrous, cavernously breathing maw, jaws agape, into which shimmering shoals of fish were vanishing, swallowed whole ...

It was a monster, a terrifying marine monster! And we can easily understand why our Father, completely forgetting his (still very recently acquired) human dignity, desperately clambered up the pine tree as far as he could, until he ran out of branches. Even in that safe place, his teeth were chattering, gripped by fear at the sight of that horrific beast rising up from the deep. With a great rasping thud, shattering shells, pebbles and coral, the monster heaved itself onto the beach and stood there on its two legs, thicker than the trunks of teak trees, its claws clogged with detritus from the marine jungle. Out of the cavern of its jaws, through its terrifying teeth, green with slime and algae, came a heavy sigh, either weary or furious, and so strong that it sent the dry seaweed and the light shells whirling up into the air. Among the stony excrescences crowning its forehead were two short, blunt, black horns. Its pale glassy eyes were like two enormous dead moons. Dragging through the sea far behind it came an immense toothed tail, its every slow swish provoking a storm.

You will already have recognized these rather

unpleasant features as belonging to the Ichthyosaurus, the most terrifying cetacean ever conceived by Jehovah. Yes, there it was—possibly the last of its kind to live on in the oceanic depths until that memorable twenty-eighth day of October—just so our Father could get a glimpse of the origins of life. And now, linking the old times with the new, there the Ichthyosaurus stood before Adam, roaring so horrendously that even the scales on its back bristled. Still clinging to the tall tree trunk, our venerable Father let out a scream of sheer horror. And then, from beside the misty lagoons, a cry or, rather, a great howl rent the air, like a fierce wind whistling down a ravine. What could it be? Another monster? Yes! The Plesiosaurus, the very last Plesiosaurus was rising up out of the swamp. And to the astonishment of the First Man (and to the delight of paleontologists), the two beasts immediately engaged in the battle that would mark the end of Earth's prehuman age. There was the fabulous head of the Plesiosaurus, with its bird's beak, sharper than the sharpest spear, its long, long, narrow neck, which undulated and arched, thrust and darted with remarkable elegance! Its soft, glutinous, shapeless, wrinkled, lichen-covered body was propelled by two incredibly strong fins. And so vast was it that, with its long neck held erect, it resembled another great black dune occupied by a solitary pine tree. It continued its furious advance. And suddenly everything was a ghastly tumult of grunts and whistles and booming thuds, whirling sand and seething seas. Our venerable Father jumped from tree to tree, trembling so much that the sturdy trunks trembled too. And when, as the roaring grew louder, he dared to look, the one thing he could make out in the roiling mass of those two monsters, through a fog of foam red with blood, was the Plesiosaurus's beak buried in the Ichthyosaurus's soft belly, while the latter's tail flailed wildly about against the backdrop of the pale, startled skies. Our venerable Father again covered his face. A monstrous, agonizing cry filled the beach. The pale dunes shook, the deep caves echoed. There then ensued a very long silence, in which the sound of the Ocean was little more than a consoling murmur of relief. Crouched among the branches, Adam peered down. The wounded Plesiosaurus was withdrawing to the warm mud of its swamps. And on the beach lay the dead Ichthyosaurus, like a hill on which the afternoon waves were gently breaking.

Then our venerable Father cautiously climbed down from his tree, and approached the dead monster. The surrounding sand was horribly churned up, full of slow streams, dark pools, steaming with newly shed blood. So vast was the Ichthyosaurus that Adam, gazing in amazement, could not even see the spines along the top of its steep side, from which the Plesiosaurus's beak had torn off scales as heavy as flagstones. However, there before his trembling hands were the gashes in the creature's soft belly, from which gushed blood and blubber, huge unravelling entrails and slivers of pink flesh ... And our venerable Father's flat nostrils grew strangely wide as they sniffed the air.

All that afternoon, as he walked from the Forest through Paradise, he had been sucking berries, gnawing roots, and munching insects with crisp shells. Now, though, the Sun was sinking into the sea, and, standing there on that beach, where he could see only wind-battered thistles, Adam felt hungry. Ah, that firm, bloody, still living flesh gave off such a fresh, salty odor! His jaws opened noisily in a bored, hungry yawn ... The Ocean was snoring as if it were asleep ...

Unable to resist, Adam stuck his fingers into one of the Ichthyosaurus's wounds, then licked and sucked them, moist with blood and flesh. The shock of this new taste immobilized this frugal man who had hitherto known only plants and fruits. Then he hurled himself on that mountain of abundance, and tore out a handful of flesh which he chewed and swallowed, grunting furiously, with an urgency that was a mixture of pleasure and fear at this, the first meat he had ever eaten.

After dining on the raw meat of that marine monster, our venerable Father felt a great thirst come upon him. The gleaming pools of water on the sand were salty. In the quiet twilight, Adam walked across the dunes and into the fields, desperately seeking some fresh water. Those universally moist times were full of babbling, fast-flowing streams. Soon, Adam was lying prone on a muddy bank taking long, consoling gulps of water, beneath the startled buzz of the phosphorescent flies that kept getting entangled in his matted hair.

The stream ran beside a forest of oak and beech trees. Night was coming on, plunging into darkness the thick undergrowth where mallows and mint and parsley mingled. Our venerable

Father entered this cool clearing, worn out from walking and from the many shocks he had experienced that afternoon in Paradise. And as soon as he stretched out on that perfumed carpet—his hairy face resting on his hands, his knees drawn up to his distended belly, tight as a drum—he fell into a deeper sleep than any he had known, a sleep peopled with shifting shadows—birds building nests, the legs of insects weaving webs, two creatures afloat on the rolling waves.

According to the Legend, in the undergrowth surrounding the First Man as he slept, twitching snouts began to appear, pricked ears, tiny eyes like shiny, jet-black buttons, restless backbones quivering with excitement, while, high up in the oaks and the beeches, there was a flutter of wings, and all kinds of beaks (curved, sharp, fierce, pensive) gleamed in the slender light of the Moon as it rose behind the hills and bathed the highest branches. Then a hyena was seen on the edge of the clearing, limping and whimpering. Across the plain came two scrawny, starving wolves, green eyes glowing. These were soon joined by the lions, their regal, gold-maned heads held high, brows proudly furrowed. Then a panting herd arrived, with the aurochs occasionally, impatiently, locking horns with the antlers of the caribou. A general shiver ran down every back when the tiger and the black panther sidled in on silent, velvet paws, blood-red tongues lolling. From the valleys, from the mountains, from the cliffs, came others, in such a hurry that the hideous primitive horses collided with the kangaroos, and the hippo-potamus's slimy snout was pressed against the dromedary's slow thighs. In among that throng of legs and hooves was an alliance of ferrets, lizards, weasels, as well as a glossy snake that swallowed the weasel, and a very happy mon-goose that promptly murdered the snake. A band of gazelles came stumbling along, grazing their slender legs on the horny backs of a long line of crocodiles, who, jaws ready and open, were lumbering, groaning, up onto the bank. Beneath the light of the Moon, the whole plain was a living, breathing rise and fall of close-knit backs from which arose now the neck of a gi-raffe, now the head of a python, like the masts of shipwrecks rocked by the waves. And finally, making the ground shake and filling the whole sky, came the hairy mastodon, its trunk curled back between its curved tusks.

For, knowing that the First Man had fallen

asleep and was lying there, utterly defenseless, the entire Animal life of Paradise had converged on that deserted forest, hoping against hope to destroy and eliminate from the Earth the Intelligent Energy that was destined to subdue Brute Force. However, out of that terrifying, steaming throng gathered on the edge of the clearing where Adam lay sleeping among the mallows and the mint, not a single beast advanced. Long, bared teeth glinted menacingly; every horn was ready to attack; every claw and hoof was pawing the soft ground; and in the treetops, every beak was pecking hungrily at the threads of moonlight … And yet no bird flew down, no beast stepped forward, because at Adam's side stood a pale, grave-faced Figure, white wings furled, hair caught back in a ring of stars, body encased in a diamond cuirass, its two gleaming hands gripping the hilt of a sword made of light—and this creature was alive.

Day was breaking with passionate pomp, communicating to the happy Earth, to the wildly happy Earth, to an Earth as yet ignorant of rags and poverty, to an Earth that knew no graves or tombs, a superior happiness, more solemn, more sacred, more nuptial. Adam awoke, and blinking heavy eyelids, surprised at this his first human awakening, he felt a soft, sweet weight pressed against him. Gripped by the terror that had never left his heart since his life among the trees, he sprang to his feet, making so much noise that the blackbirds, nightingales and warblers, all the little birds of celebration and love, woke up too and burst into a song full of jollity and hope. For, O wonder, there before Adam, as if it were both him and not him, was another Being—very similar to him, only more slender and covered with a more silken down—regarding him with wide, lustrous, liquid eyes. Its thick, blonde, reddish-blonde hair fell in thick waves down to its full, rounded, fecund thighs. Between its downy folded arms were two plump, abundant breasts the color of an arbutus fruit, their firm, tumescent nipples adorned with a curly down. And slowly, gently rubbing its bare knees together, the whole of this silken, tender Being was offering itself up in astonished, lascivious submission. It was Eve ... It was you, O Venerable Mother!

Chapter III

Then began the abominable days of Paradise.

Our Parents' tireless, desperate efforts were devoted entirely to surviving in the midst of a Nature that was ceaselessly, furiously plotting their destruction. And Adam and Eve spent those days—which Semitic texts celebrate as delightful—always trembling, always whimpering, always fleeing! The Earth was very much a work in progress, and the Divine Energy, which was still in the process of creating it, was constantly making emendations, changing its mind so often that a place, which, at dawn, had been covered by a forest had become, by night, a lagoon in which the already ailing Moon had come to study its own pale face. Many a time, our Parents, resting on the slope of an innocent hill among the rosemary and the thyme (Adam resting his head on Eve's thigh, and Eve, with her nimble fingers, looking for nits in Adam's hair) were sent tumbling down that gentle slope, amid the rumble and the flames and the smoke and the gray ash of the volcano that Jehovah had just that minute created, as if they had been shaken off the back of some highly irritable creature! Many a night, they would escape, howling, from some cosy cave, as a great roaring swell of sea broke over it and lay seething among the rocks, with the corpses of black seals floating on the surface. Or else it was the ground, the supposedly safe ground, already civilized into friendly, fertile fields, that would suddenly roar like some wild beast and become a bottomless maw swallowing flocks, meadows, springs, as well as beneficent cedars along with the turtle-doves cooing in their branches.

Then there was the rain, the long Edenic rain, falling in clamorous torrents for long deluge-filled days and teeming, drenching nights, rain so abundant that all that could be seen of Paradise, now a vast muddy pond, were the tips of drowned trees and the peaks of mountains crammed with creatures howling in terror at the all-consuming waters. And our Parents would sit perched on a high rock, uttering mournful moans, with rivers of rain streaming down their backs and legs as if the new clay from which Jehovah had made them were already dissolving.

The summers were even more terrifying. Nothing could compare with those droughts in Paradise! Slow sad day after slow sad day, the immense red-hot ember of the searing Sun bore furiously down from a copper-colored sky as the thick, dull air crackled and heaved. In the heat, great crevasses and fissures appeared in the mountains, and the plains vanished beneath a blackened layer of twisted, tangled threads, hard as wire, which was what remained of the green pastures. The scorched foliage was blown about by the burning winds, more roar than rustle. The beds of the desiccated rivers were as hard as smelted iron. The moss hung from the rocks like dry skin peeling off huge bones. Every night, a forest burned like a sputtering bonfire of parched wood, scalding the vault of that inclement oven. All of Eden was covered in flocks of vultures and crows, because, with so many animals dying from hunger and thirst, there was an abundance of rotting meat. The little water that remained in the river barely moved, chockablock with a churning mass of snakes, frogs, otters, turtles seeking refuge in that last warm, muddy vein of water. And our venerable Parents—bony ribs heaving against their burnt skin, their tongues as hard as cork—wandered from spring to spring, desperately drinking any rare drops that still bubbled up and sizzled on the scalding stones ...

So it was that Adam and Eve began life in the Garden of Delights, fleeing Fire, fleeing Water, fleeing Earth, and fleeing Air.

And in the midst of these continual, manifest dangers, they had to eat! Ah, eating, what a major enterprise that was for our venerable Parents! Especially since Adam (and later Eve too, initiated by Adam), once he had experienced the fatal pleasures of meat, could no longer find flavor or satisfaction or indeed dignity in the fruit, roots and berries of his Animal existence. Not that there was a shortage of good meat in Paradise. The salmon of those primitive times would have been delicious, but they were in the rapids, happily swimming. The water rail or the flamboyant pheasant, both fed on the grains the Creator had deemed good, would have been tasty too, but they were smug and safe up in the skies. And the rabbits and the hares were always scampering off through the scented undergrowth! And our Father, in those innocent days, had neither fishhook nor arrow. This is why he was ceaselessly patrolling the lagoons and the seashore in case some dead cetacean might have washed up there. These rich finds, however, were rare, and on their hungry tramps along banks and shores, the glum human couple would perhaps find, here and there, on the rocks or in the scumbled sand, an ugly crab on whose hard shell they would cut their lips. These deserted shores were also infested with packs of wild beasts waiting, like Adam, for the waves to carry in any fishes defeated by storms or killed in battle. And how often did our Parents, just as they were biting into a slice of seal or dolphin, have to flee disconsolately on hearing the soft steps of some dread troglodyte or the heavy breath of the polar bears swaying along the white sand, beneath the white indifference of the Moon!

It's true, though, that their hereditary tree-climbing knowledge often helped our Parents in their hunt for food. If, beneath the branches of the cinnamon tree where they perched, slyly watching, a stray goat or a young, inexperienced tortoise should come stumping through the short grass, they knew what a feast was theirs! They would tear a goat to pieces in a trice, and, in a frenzy, suck its blood: and our strong Mother Eve, uttering somber squeals, would wrench off the legs of a tortoise, one by one, reaching beneath its shell. However, on many other nights, after anguishing periods of no food at all, Earth's Chosen Ones were forced to drive off a hyena with angry shouts, pursuing it through the forest, in order to steal from it a fetid, drool-covered bone, the remnant of a dead lion! And worse days followed, when hunger reduced our Parents to resorting to the grim frugality of their time in the Trees—eating weeds and green shoots and bitter roots—thus experiencing in the abundance of Paradise, the very first Poverty!

And throughout these travails, they never lost their terror of wild beasts. For while Adam and Eve dined on the easy prey of weaker animals, they, too, were the favored prey of the larger beasts. Eating Eve, so round and plump, was doubtless the dream of many a tiger lurking in the reedbeds of Paradise. Many a bear, even while engaged in stealing honeycombs from a hole in the trunk of an oak tree, would pause and tremble and lick its lips, when, suddenly filled with a longing for something more refined, it spotted through the branches, caught in a ray of sunlight, the muscular body of our venerable Father! And danger did not come only from the starving hordes of carnivores, but from the slow, sated, idle herbivores, the aurochs, the wild oxen, the stags, who would happily gore or trample our Parents out of sheer stupidity, simply because they did not like the look or smell of them. To which were added those who killed in order not to be killed themselves, because life in Paradise was ruled by the laws of Fear, Hunger and Fury.

True, our Parents were also fierce and tremendously strong, and expert at the useful art of climbing to the leafy tops of trees, but the leopard could, with more confident, feline skill, leap soundlessly from branch to branch. The boa constrictor, too, could reach the highest branches of the tallest cedar to pick off monkeys, and with a snake's obtuse inability to distinguish the very different qualities hidden beneath an apparently similar form, could easily have swallowed Adam. And what use were Adam's hands, even working in alliance with Eve's hands, against the terrifying lions in the Garden of Delights, which Zoology, still not without a shudder, calls *Leo anticus*? Or against the primitive hyenas who were so bold that, in the early days of Genesis, the Angels, when they came down to Paradise, would always walk around with their wings folded, in case the hyenas should leap out at them from the bamboo and rip off their shining feathers? Or against the dogs, those formidable dogs of Paradise, who, attacking as they did in dense, howling packs, were, in the early days of Man's existence, his very worst enemies!

And in the midst of that threatening animal life, Adam had not a single ally. His own relatives, the envious, mocking Anthropoids, would pelt him with giant coconuts. Only one creature, and a redoubtable one at that, felt a certain slow, majestic sympathy for Man. This was the Mastodon. However, in those Edenic days, our Father's still rather hazy intelligence did not comprehend the kindness and justice, the obliging nature of that admirable pachyderm. And thus it was that, during those tragic early years, Adam lived in a permanent state of terror, with his own weakness and isolation as his one certainty, a state so enduring and so persistent that his fear, like a prolonged shudder, was passed on to his progeny, and it is Adam's ancient fear that still, even in the safest forest, fills us with unease whenever we go for a solitary evening stroll.

And let us not forget that, among the polite, rational creatures in Paradise, ready to appear in M. de Buffon's noble prose, there were still a few of the grotesque monsters that sullied Creation before the purifying dawn of that twenty-fifth day of October. Jehovah did, however, spare Adam the degrading horror of living in Paradise in the company of that hideous monstrosity to which astonished paleontologists gave the name Iguanodon! On the eve of Man's arrival, Jehovah, very charitably, drowned the Iguanodons in a swamp, in a remote corner of Paradise, now modern-day Flanders. However, Adam and Eve were familiar with the Pterodactyls. Ah, those Pterodactyls! They had the body of a scaly, feathery alligator, two dark, sinister, fleshy bat wings, and a huge, gaping beak the length of their body and full of hundreds of teeth as sharp as those of a saw. They would fall upon their prey and smother it with those soft, silent wings, as if with a sticky, ice-cold cloth, then tear it to pieces with a violent gnashing of their fetid mandibles. And there were as many of these bizarre gigantic birds darkening the sky of Paradise as there are blackbirds and swallows filling the blessed skies of Portugal. They were a blight on the days of our venerable Parents, whose poor hearts never beat faster than when they saw flying in from beyond the mountains, with a sinister clatter of wings and beaks, a whole flock of Pterodactyls.

How did our Parents survive in that Garden of Delights? The glittering sword of the Angel guarding them certainly had a lot of work to do!

But you see, my friends, Man owes his triumphant career to those furious beings. Without the Saurians and the Pterodactyls, and the primitive hyenas, and the shiver of terror they spread around them, as well as the need to come up with a rational defense against their bestial attacks, the Earth would have remained a fear-filled Paradise, where we would all be wandering the seashore, naked and disheveled, hoping to find some beached monster on whose raw flesh we could gorge ourselves. We, his descendants, owe our supremacy to Adam's cowering terror. It was thanks to those bestial threats that he was obliged to climb up to the highest peaks of Humanity. The Mesopotamian poets of Genesis revealed their understanding of Man's origins in those subtle verses in which the Serpent, that most dangerous of creatures, leads Adam, out of love for Eve, to eat the fruit of the Tree of Knowledge. If the troglodyte Lion had never roared, Man would not now be working in cities, because Civilization was born out of his desperate attempts to defend himself against both the Unfeeling and the Unthinking. Society is really the work of the wild beasts. If, in Paradise, the Hyena and the Tiger had begun languidly stroking Adam's hairy back with a friendly paw, Adam would have become the friend of the Tiger and the Hyena, sharing their lairs, their prey, their idleness, and their savage tastes. And the Intelligent Energy that had brought him down from the Tree would soon have dissipated in that inert brutish state, much as a spark, even in a pile of dry twigs, will not survive long enough to overcome the cold and the dark if extinguished by a chill wind whistling in through a dark hole.

However, one afternoon (as the very precise Jacobus Usserius Armachanus would later teach us), when Adam and Eve were emerging from the gloom of a forest, a huge bear, the Father of All Bears, appeared before them, raised its black paws and opened wide its bloodthirsty jaws ... Then, trapped and with no escape, and determined to defend his woman, the Father of Mankind hurled the stick he was leaning on—a sturdy branch found in the forest and which ended in a very sharp point—at that Father of All Bears ...and the point pierced the bear's heart.

Ah, ever since that blessed afternoon, Man has truly existed on the Earth.

He became a Man, and a superior one, when

he took one terrified step forward, extracted the stick from the dead monster's breast and looked at the wound spouting blood, frowning in his efforts to understand. Then his eyes shone brightly at this astounding victory. He had understood ...

Not even bothering to eat the bear's sound flesh, Adam raced back into the forest and spent the rest of the afternoon, for as long as daylight lasted, tearing off branches from trees, very carefully and skillfully, so that one end always had a good sharp point. Ah, what a splendid sound of tearing rang through the forest, through the cool shade, in celebration of that first Redemptive act! You, friendly forest, the very first workshop, who knows where you now lie in your ancient tomb, transformed into black coal! When, positively steaming with sweat, our venerable Parents left the trees and returned to their distant lair, they were stooped beneath the glorious weight of two great bundles of spears.

After that, there was no end to Man's prowess. The crows and jackals had not even had time to strip the flesh from that Father of All Bears' carcass when *our* Father had already split in two the end of his victorious stick, and placed in the resulting fork one of those very sharp pointed stones that had sometimes bruised his feet when he went down to the river, tying it tightly in place with an ivy vine. And there you have the first spear! Since those stones were not so very common, Adam and Eve made their fingers bleed trying to split the hard round pebbles into slivers, which, with their sharp ends and edges, were perfect for scraping and piercing. The stone resisted, reluctant to help the Man who, in the Genesic days of that great October, it had tried to supplant (according to the prodigious Chronicles of Baktun). Another idea lit up Adam's face, an idea that burned through him like a spark straight from the Eternal Wisdom. He picked up a large rock and struck the stone, which promptly split into splinters. And there you have the first hammer!

On another fortunate afternoon, while walking across a dark, bare hill, he spotted—with those eyes that were now constantly seeking and comparing—a black stone, rough and faceted and with a dull sheen to it. He was amazed at how heavy it was, and immediately sensed that it could prove to be a better, much harder hammer. Clutching it to him, he excitedly carried it off to batter that rebellious flint stone. Eve was waiting for him by the river, where he immediately brought the stone down hard on the flint. Horrors! A spark flew up, glowed and died! Both of them recoiled and exchanged terrified, almost awestruck looks. His hands had produced from that unhewn rock a very bright spark, similar in brightness to the light that shines down from among the clouds. Trembling, Adam struck again. Another spark, which, again, died, and Adam, mystified, studied the dark stone from every angle, even sniffing it. Our venerable Parents, their hair buffeted by the wind, made their way thoughtfully back to their usual cave on the slope of a hill, next to a spring bubbling up among the ferns.

And there, in their cave, Adam, filled with a curiosity pulsating with hope, placed the piece of stone—the size of a pumpkin—between his calloused feet and started hammering again, while Eva knelt beside him and kept blowing. Again, a spark leapt up, glimmered in the darkness, as brightly as those shimmering lights gazing down on them from the heavens. However, while those lights remained alive in the dark sky, keeping radiant watch throughout the night, the tiny stars springing up from the stone died almost the moment they were born. Was it the wind that carried them off, the same wind that carries off everything, voices, clouds, leaves? Our venerable Father, fleeing the malevolent wind whistling round the hill, withdrew into the most sheltered part of the cave, where they had their bed composed of layers of soft, dry straw. And again he struck the rock, sending up spark after spark, while Eve crouched down, protecting those fiery, fleeting beings with her hands. A whisper of smoke curled up from the straw, growing ever thicker, followed by a red flame ... Fire! Terrified, our Parents rushed out of the cave, which was now filled with sweet-smelling smoke, among which danced joyful, glittering tongues of flame that licked the cave walls. Crouched at the entrance to their lair, their eyes watering from the acrid smoke, both were breathing hard and feeling, in equal parts, astonished and alarmed by what they had created. And yet, despite their alarm and shock, they felt a very new and penetrating sweetness, which had its origin in that light and that warmth ... The smoke had now vanished from the cave, carried off by the thieving wind. The flames burned lower now, bluer and more hesitant; soon, all that was left were a few fading, graying embers slowly dissolving into ash, until the last glow flickered and faded. The fire had died! Then into Adam's nascent Soul came a terrible, ruinous grief. His thick lips quivered and he sobbed. Would he ever be able to recreate that marvelous thing? And our Mother, already assuming her role as consoler-in-chief, consoled him. With clumsy, nervous hands—for she was about to perform her first task—she made another pile of dry straw, on top of which she placed the round flint stone, then picking up the dark rock, she struck the flint hard, sending up tiny starlike sparks. And again the smoke curled up, and again the flame burned bright. Success! There was the first fire in Paradise, and not one that had happened by chance, but had been ignited by a very clear-sighted Will, which now, and for ever after, every night and every morning, would confidently repeat that supreme task.

The sweet, august task of creating fire belonged then to our venerable Mother. She created it, fed it, defended it, and preserved it. And like any besotted mother, each day she discovered in that resplendent child a new virtue or beauty. Adam knew then that it was *her* fire that drove away the wild beasts, and that, finally, they had a safe place to hide, *their* safe place. Not only safe, but pleasant too, because a fire lights and warms and heats and cheers and cleanses. And when Adam, with a sheaf of spears, went down to the plain or into the forest to hunt, he did so with renewed energy, so that he could return as soon as possible to the safety and consolation of the fire. Ah, how sweet it was, that penetrating warmth, drying the cold dew from his skin, and filling his craggy home with golden light, like the light from the Sun! More than that, it delighted and enchanted his eyes, sending him into fertile reveries, in which, inspired, he saw the shapes of arrows, hammers with handles, curved bones for catching fish, serrated stones that cut through wood! And Adam owed those creative moments to his strong wife!

And what a debt the whole of Humanity owes her! Let us remember, brothers and sisters, that our Mother, with the superior instinct that, later, made her Prophetess and Sibyl, did not hesitate when the Serpent, coiled among the Roses, said to her: "Eat of the fruit of the Tree of Knowledge and your eyes will be opened, and you will be like the Gods, knowing good and evil!" Adam would have preferred to eat that very juicy Serpent. He didn't believe in fruit that could make you Godlike and Wise. After all, he had eaten plenty of fruit from the trees and had remained as ignorant and beast-like as the bear or the aurochs. Eve, however, with the sublime credulity that always brings about the world's most sublime transformations, immediately ate the Apple, peel and pips and all. And in persuading Adam to share that Transcendental Apple, she very sweetly and slyly convinced him of the advantages, the happiness, the glory, and the power that Knowledge brings! This allegory written by the poets of Genesis reveals to us with splendid subtlety the great work that Eve carried out in those painful years in Paradise. Through her, God continued his work of Creation, that of building the spiritual Kingdom, which, here on Earth, became home, family, tribe, city. It was Eve who laid the foundation stones on which Humanity is built.

If you don't agree, consider this. When the brave hunter returns to the cave bent beneath the weight of his dead prey and smelling of grass and blood and beast, he was doubtless the one to skin the creature with a stone knife, to slice it up, strip the bones (which he eagerly hid away for his own consumption, full as they were of precious bone marrow). Eve, meanwhile, added those skins to the others she had stored up, keeping to one side any broken bones because their sharp points could be used to pierce and puncture, and stashing any leftover meat in a cavity in the rock face. On one occasion, she accidentally dropped one of those large slabs of meat and it fell near the fire which she now kept permanently lit. The flames spread, slowly licking the fatty part of the flesh, and a delicious, unfamiliar smell reached the nose of our venerable Mother. Where was that tempting smell coming from? From the fire, where the slice of deer meat or hare was now grilling and sizzling. Then Eve, grave-faced and inspired, placed the meat on the hot flames, and waited, kneeling, before spearing it with one end of a bone to remove it from the crackling flames, and somberly, silently biting into it. Her shining eyes announced yet another discovery. And with the same loving haste with which she had offered Adam the Apple, she now presented him with this new meat, which he sniffed at suspiciously, then tore into with his teeth, grunting with pleasure! And so it was that, with that piece of roast venison, our Parents victoriously climbed up another rung on the ladder of Humanity!

They still drank from the nearby spring among the ferns, mouths pressed to the clear water. After drinking, Adam leaned on his sturdy spear and stared off into the distance at the slowly flowing river, at the mountains crowned with snow or light, at the Sun glittering on the sea, and in his ponderous way he wondered if the hunting might be better over there or the forests less dense. Eve, on the other hand, went straight back to the cave in order to immerse herself in the task she loved best. Sitting cross-legged on the floor, her curly head bowed, our Mother was using a sharp piece of bone to make small holes along the edge of a piece of animal skin, and repeating this process along the edge of another skin. She was so absorbed in this work that she didn't even hear Adam coming in and rummaging around among his various weapons, but, instead, concentrated on joining those two skins together by passing through the holes a slender thread taken from the seaweed left to dry in front of the fire. Adam viewed this trivial work with disdain, for it added nothing to his strength. He did not yet realize, our brutish Father, that those skins, once sewn together, would provide protection for his body, the framework for his tent, the bag for his provisions, the canteen for his water, and the drum he would beat when he became a Warrior, as well as the page on which he would write when he became a Prophet!

He found other interests and habits of hers equally irritating, and sometimes, with an already all-too-human lack of humanity, our Father would grab his wife by the hair, throw her to the ground, and kick her with his calloused feet. He was seized by just such a rage one afternoon when he found Eve sitting by the fire with a little puppy on her lap, still very unsteady on its feet, and which she was teaching to gnaw on a piece of fresh meat. She had found the puppy lost and cold and whimpering by the side of the spring, and, having very gently picked it up, had provided it with warmth and food, and this filled her with a very pleasing emotion that brought a smile, a maternal smile, to her thick lips, lips that, as yet, barely knew how to smile. Our venerable Father, eyes glinting, reached out as if to kill and devour the puppy that had dared to enter his lair, but Eve defended the small trembling creature now fondly licking her. This was the very first example on Earth of Charity—as formless as the first flower that sprang up from the mud! And in the short harsh words that made up our Parents' language, she tried to convince Adam that it would be helpful to have a friendly beast living with them in their cave ... Adam bit his lip. Then he gently ran his fingers over the soft back of the cowering little pup. And this was a major moment in History! Man domesticates Beast! From that puppy living snugly in Paradise would come the dog as man's friend, man's alliance with the horse, and subsequently his dominion over the sheep. The flock would grow; the shepherd would herd it; and the faithful dog would keep guard. Eve, sitting by her fire, was preparing the ground for the wandering tribes grazing their cattle.

Then, during the long mornings when wild Adam was out hunting, Eve would wander from valley to mountain, picking up shells, birds' eggs, strange roots, and seeds, purely for the pleasure of collecting things and filling her lair with new treasures, which she would hide in crevices in the cave wall. One day, when she was near the spring, a handful of seeds had fallen through her fingers onto the damp, black earth. A green shoot later appeared, a stem pushing up through the soil, and then an ear of wheat ripened. Its grains tasted good. Intrigued, Eve buried more seeds, hoping to create around their cave a little patch of tall grasses that would produce ears of wheat and bring her more sweet, tender grains … And there you have the first wheat field! And thus our Mother, in deepest Paradise, sowed the seeds for the settled tribes who would one day work the land.

Meanwhile, we can safely assume that Abel was born and that, one by one, the days slipped by in Paradise, so much safer now and easier. The volcanoes were slowly fizzling out. The cliffs no longer collapsed with a rumble and a roar onto the innocent abundance of the valleys below. The rivers were now so meek and mild that the clouds and the branches of the elm trees would spend hours gazing at their own reflections in the rivers' transparent depths. Only on very rare occasions did a Pterodactyl, with its scandalously long beak and wings, darken the sky in which the Sun alternated with mist, and the summers were interspersed with light rain showers. And there was, in this growing tranquility, something like a conscious feeling of submission. The World sensed and accepted Man's supremacy. The forests no longer burned like stubble, because they knew that Man would soon require from them a stake, a beam, an oar, a mast. The wind blowing down the narrow ravines grew more disciplined, rehearsing the regular gusts that would set the grindstone of the windmill working. The sea had drowned its monsters, and now lay supine in preparation for the keels of ships that would one day cut through it. The Earth subdued its fields and gently moistened them, in readiness for the plow and the seed. And the various metals were happily lined up ready for the fire that would give them shape and beauty.

And in the evenings, Adam returned home contented, his bag full of game. The fire flickered and lit up the face of our Father, whom Life and the effort of living had made more handsome, his lips less prominent, his head filled now with slow thoughts, his eyes brighter and less restless. The lamb roasting on a spit over the fire oozed and sizzled. On the ground there were coconut shells full of clear spring water. To their bed, now made of ferns, they had added the comfort of a bearskin. Another similar skin hung over the entrance to the cave. One corner, now the workshop, was full of piles of flints and a hammer; another corner had become the arsenal, where Adam kept his spears and cudgels. Eve was busy spinning wool from goat hair. Abel, plump and naked, his pale skin covered by a very light down, was asleep by the warmth of the fire, on a bed of dry leaves. Sharing both bed and warmth was the dog, now fully grown, and he, with his snout resting on his paws, was keeping fond watch over Abel. Adam, meanwhile, was absorbed in a very strange task, using the point of a sharp stone to engrave on a large piece of bone the antlers, back, and outstretched legs of a deer running! The wood on the fire crackled. All the stars in the sky were now present and correct. Meanwhile, God was thoughtfully contemplating the gradual growth of Humankind.

And now that I have lit this real fire with dry branches from the Tree of Knowledge, in the starry night of Paradise, allow me to leave you, O venerable Parents!

I no longer fear that the ever-shifting Earth will crush you, or that the large beasts will devour you, or that the Energy that brought you from the Forest will burn out, like a faulty lamp, and send you back to your Tree. You are now irremediably human, and each morning you will progress with such speed and impetus toward the perfection of the Body and the glory of the Mind, that soon—in the space of a few hundreds and thousands of years—Eve will be Helen and Adam the great Aristotle.

However, I am not entirely sure whether I should congratulate you, O venerable Parents! Some of your other brothers stayed among the dense trees, and lead a very pleasant life.

Every morning, the Orangutan wakes in his bed of leaves, on a soft mattress of moss carefully arranged by him on a couch of perfumed branches. Languidly, with not a care in the world, he lingers idly on the soft moss, listening to the limpid songs of the birds, savoring the rays of sunlight filtering through the lacework of leaves, and licking the sugar-sweet dew from the hair on his arms. Later, after much scratching and rubbing, he climbs lazily up to his favorite tree, especially chosen from among the others for its coolness and for the lulling elasticity of its branches. Then, having breathed in the aroma-laden breezes, he leaps nimbly through the ever-open, ever-full larders of the forest, breakfasting on bananas, mangos, and guavas, the fine fruits that render him as healthy and immune to disease as the trees he picked them from. Then, in a sociable mood, he strolls along the forest's lively streets and alleyways; he plays with clever friends, amicable games requiring skill and strength; he flirts with the kindly lady Orangutans, who groom him and then, swaying and talking, hang beside him on some flower-heavy liana; with another happy band of friends he trots along the banks of the clear rivers, or, perched on one end of a branch, listens to a talkative old chimpanzee telling amusing tales of hunting, travel, love, and about the many tricks he has played on those poor earthbound creatures unable to climb trees. He returns early to his own tree and, reclining in his leafy hammock, he abandons himself to the delights of dreaming—a waking dream, similar to our Metaphysics and our Epics, but which, being based entirely on real sensations, unlike our own uncertain dreams, is a dream full of certainties. The Forest slowly falls silent, night slips in among the tree trunks, and the happy Orangutan goes back to his bed of leaves and moss, and falls asleep in God's vast peace, a God he has never bothered to name, still less deny, and yet who still rains down on him, with impartial fondness, the wonders of his Mercy.

This is how the Orangutan fills his day in the Trees. How, then, did Man, the Orangutan's cousin, spend his day in the City? Suffering, because he possesses the superior gifts that the Orangutan does not! Suffering, because he must forever drag around with him that incurable disease, his Soul! Suffering, because our Father Adam, on that terrible twenty-eighth day of October, having seen and smelled Paradise, did not dare to say to his Lord very respectfully: "Thank you, gentle Creator, but give the government of the Earth to whoever you think best qualified, to the Elephant or the Kangaroo, because, very wisely, I am going back to my Tree!"

However, since our venerable Father had neither the foresight nor the gumption to say No to the Supreme Being, we continue to reign over Creation as sublime beings ... Above all, we continue to make insatiable use of the best of the many gifts that God gave us, the purest and the one truly great gift, the gift of loving Him, even if He didn't also grant us the gift of understanding Him. And let us not forget that He taught us, in those raised voices in Galilee, and beneath the mango trees in Veluvana, and in the harsh valleys of Yen Chao, that the best way of loving Him is to love each other, and to love His work, even the worms and the rocks and the poisonous roots, and even those vast beings that do not seem to need our love, those Suns, those Worlds, those scattered Nebulae, which, like us, were once held in God's hand and formed out of the same substance as us, and which certainly do not love us—indeed, they may not even know that we exist.